Lulu the Lion Cub Learns to Roar

JAIME AMOR

A COSMIC KIDS! YOGA ADVENTURE

WATKINS

Sharing Wisdom Since
1893

Today we are off to meet Lulu the lion cub
in Tanzania in Africa. Yay!

Just copy the moves in the pictures
and enjoy the adventure.

Let's get ready . . .

Someone's coming on the journey with you!
Can you find the Greg the grasshopper hiding
in every picture?

Sit on the floor and cross your legs. Bring your hands together in front of your heart.

Now bow forward and say our yoga code word, "Na-ma-stay", which joins us all together.

Namaste!
Hello!

We need to get our body ready for the long plane journey to Tanzania.

Let's start by warming up our neck!

Turn your head and look to one side . . .

. . . and then to the other side.

Nod your head all the way forward and all the way up. Again, all the way forward and all the way up!

We will need to carry a backpack,
so let's warm up our shoulders too.

> *Roll your shoulders round and round.*

> *Then lift them both up and put them down. Lift them up and put them down.*

> *Lift up one, lift up two, put down one, put down two. Again! Up, up, down, down, up, up, down, down . . .*

5

Right, grab your backpack and let's get to the airport.
It's time to catch a **plane**.

Fly like a plane! Come up on your knees and stretch your arms out.

Drop one hand down to the floor next to you. Lift the other arm to the sky like the wing of a plane.

Neowwww!

If your plane is flying well, bring the top foot in front of your knee.

Then stretch your other leg out behind you. Lift your hips and go, "Neowwww!"

Neowwww!

Fly your plane on the other side. Come back to your knees and stretch your arms wide.

Phew. It's a very long journey!

Neowwww!

Drop one hand down to the floor next to you. Then lift the other arm to the sky.

If you did it on the first side, bring your top foot in front of your knee and stretch your other leg out behind you.

Our plane has arrived in Tanzania at last.
Wow! It's really hot here so we had better
put on some **sun cream**.

*Blob some
sun cream on
your hands and
rub it all the way
down your legs and
all the way up.*

Blob,
blob,
blob!

*Don't forget
to rub some
cream on
your face!*

Now get in the **jeep** and start the engine.

*Sit with your legs
stretched out in front
of you and hold the
steering wheel. Bump
and bend your legs as
you drive along.*

Brrm brrrrrrmmmmm!

The road is a dusty track. It's full of potholes and really bumpy so we are bounced around, leaning to one side . . .

. . . and then to the other.

Then we go down a hill . . .

. . . and up a hill.

Brrm brrrrrrmmmmm!

At last we get to our campsite and we have to put up our **tent**.

Doop!

Doop!

Doop!

Doop!

Stand up feet together, arms by your side. Then step one foot out – one tent pole. Step your second foot out – that's two poles. Lift one arm over your head – three poles. Lift the other arm – four poles. Put your hands together to give your tent a nice, pointy roof!

Now let's check the zip works!

Grab the zip at the top of the tent and slowly fold forward, your arms still stretched out. Reach down to the ground.

Ziiiip!

Great, the zip works! Now, does it go up again?

Start to pull up the zip and stop when you are halfway.

Ooops!

The zip is stuck!
Let's have another try!

Fold down to the ground again. Then lift up and stop when you are halfway.

It's got stuck again!
Let's try one more time.

Ziiiip!

Fold down and then lift up all the way to the top.

The zip works this time.
Phew! Thank goodness for that.

We have been travelling all day and we are a bit dusty and dirty. There's a river nearby so we can wash our clothes. The water rushes and roars, tossing the clothes around like a **washing machine**.

Come and sit by the river with your legs crossed. Criss-cross your fingers and put them behind your head.

Now spin your body from side to side.

Wishy washy
Wishy washy
Wishy washy wooo

Let's dry our clothes by the fire with **tumble-dryer** fingers.

Bring your pointing fingers in front of your mouth and spin them around each other. Blow on your fingers to dry your washing.

13

It's been a very long day and we are so **tired**!

Yawn!

Sit with
your legs
crossed and
stretch your
arms.

If we want to get up early in the morning to meet Lulu, we need to get some sleep. Let's **crawl** into the tent . . .

Come onto your hands and knees. Stretch one leg behind you. Stretch the opposite arm in front.

Swap your leg and arm to crawl forward.

. . . and get all **snuggly** in your sleeping bag.

Lie on your side with one elbow under your head.

In the morning we are woken by the sound
of birds **tweeting** in the trees.

*Tweet like a
bird! Come up
onto your knees
and stretch your
arms wide.*

*Then wrap
your arms
around your
shoulders. Tweet
your elbows up
and down.*

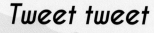

Tweet tweet
Tweet tweet

Stretch your arms wide and wrap them the other way. Tweet your elbows up and down.

Wow, the birds here make a lot of noise! It must be time to get up.

We crawl out of the tent into the fresh air and sunshine.

Look who's here.
It's Lulu the lion cub . . .
and she's singing a song!

LULU'S SONG roar

The sun is shining in the sky,
Today could be my day.
I will never give up on my dreams,
I know I will find a way.

I may only be a little cub
But I know I have got so much more,
So I take a deep breath,
I believe in myself and I do my very best roar!

Sometimes I can be unkind
And that's no way to be.
So when I feel frustration rising . . .
I tell myself to breathe!

I will never give up and I will learn as I go
And I will pick myself up off the floor.
So I take a deep breath,
I believe in myself and I do my very best roar!

Roar like a lion and shake the ground
There's a fire in my heart and it's got to come out
If I can roar like a lion I have no doubt
That I will stand tall even if I am small.
RoAAARRRR!

"Hello!" says Lulu.
Let's say hello to Lulu like a **lion**.

Kneel down. Count to 3 and then rise up on your knees, bringing your hands up to your ears.

Open your mouth wide and stick out your tongue.

Hello Lulu!

"Hello!" she says again. "My name's Lulu. I don't know how to roar and everyone keeps making fun of me. I got really angry this morning, so I came for a little walk to cool off . . .

"It's so nice that you are here. Maybe you can help me learn to roar . . . "

Oh dear. Lulu doesn't seem very happy.

What can we do to help her roar?

Let's climb a **tree**. Lulu will stay at the bottom of the tree and roar as loud as she can.

We will listen out for her roar.

Stand straight like a tree and place the heel of one foot on the other foot.

Bring your hands together at your heart.

Grow your branches high into the sky. Can you stand tall and count to 10?

If your tree is really strong, try moving your foot further up your leg.

As you get good at balancing, you can raise your foot higher up your thigh. Can you still balance . . . and listen out for Lulu's roar?

21

Meanwhile Lulu gets herself ready to give her **roar** a try.

Come onto your knees.

Count to 3 and then rise up on your knees, bringing your hands up to your ears.

Open your mouth wide and stick out your tongue.

Lulu does her best, but . . . oh dear, poor Lulu! Nothing comes out . . . apart from her tongue!

22

Maybe we will hear her better if we try doing **tree** on the other side?

Swapping sides, place the heel of one foot on the other foot. Bring your hands to your heart.

Grow your branches high into the sky.

Try moving your foot up your leg toward your knee and up to your thigh.

Once again Lulu tries her best roar. But . . . it's no good! We still can't hear her.

Lulu is really angry.

"I'm never going to be able to roar. I'm so, so bad at roaring, it's horrible!" she shouts.

We know that getting angry is not going to fix anything. So we help her to stop. "You need to calm down, Lulu. Let's take some **deep breaths**. It will help us all relax."

Sit on your knees. Breathe in a big breath. Breathe out. Breathe in, breathe out. Breathe in, and out.

Aaah!

That feels better. Now we can think clearly again . . . and that's when we get another idea!

We take Lulu to the river to find Ernie the baby **elephant**. Ernie can make a really big trumpeting sound with his trunk. Maybe he can help Lulu.

Aaahoorrrr! Aaaaahoooorrr

Stand like an elephant with your legs out wide. Stretch one arm out in front like a trunk.

Lift your trunk up to the sky like a trumpeting elephant. Then swing it down between your legs.

Lulu would love to make a sound as big as Ernie. She tries to copy him and gets ready to roar . . .

1, 2, 3 . . .

But she only manages a funny little trumpet sound!

25

Lulu is very angry that Ernie can make a bigger sound than her!
Before we know what's happening she has tied his trunk in a **knot**!

Poor Ernie!

Stand tall, with your legs apart. Scissor one arm over the other.

Then bend both arms and try to make your palms touch.

"What did you do that for?" asks Ernie sadly. He's upset that his trunk is all tied up and he can't breathe very well!

"You can't do that, Lulu!" we tell the lion cub.

Lulu is not behaving very nicely.

She needs to stop getting so angry.
We help her by **counting down**
from the angry feeling.

10 9 8 7 6 5 4 3 2 1

Sit on your heels. Count slowly from 10 to 1.

At the end, take a big deep breath in and out.

Aaah!

Lulu says sorry for being so mean and taking her anger
out on poor Ernie. She carefully unties his trunk.

"Thanks, Lulu!" says Ernie.
"I'm sorry, Ernie!" Lulu says again.

Just then, Mindy the baby chimp **jumps** down from a tree.

Jump up and come down to land in a crouch.

Ooooo oooo oooo ahhh ahhh ahhh!

Mindy says, "Lulu, I heard you say that you can't roar. Why don't you do what I do? I do big monkey **jumps** with a big monkey call at the top. Like this, right?"

Jump like Mindy. Start in a crouching position and count 1,2, 3, keeping very still. Then leap up, stretching your arms and legs out.

Oooo oooo oooo ahhh ahhh ahhh!

Lulu copies her. Maybe Mindy is right and this will help Lulu to roar loudly.

This time when you jump, make a lion face and hands. Do 3 jumps.

Lulu does really good, big jumps, but she does not quite manage to roar . . .

She is still feeling a bit grumpy, but the monkey jumps were a lot of fun and she's finding it hard to stay angry.

All of a sudden, George the baby **giraffe** comes trotting round the corner.

Stand up tall and take one step forward, one step back.

Reach your hands up high to make a long giraffe neck.

George has something important to say. He folds forward, leaning down to whisper to Lulu.

In your giraffe pose, fold forward.

George whispers, "Lulu, you need to warn everyone. The volcano is about to erupt!"

Oh no! This is serious. Lulu needs to learn how to roar right now!

Lulu does not panic. She races up the nearest hill. At the top she gets herself ready.

Kneel with your hands on your legs and get ready . . .

Then she takes a big breath . . . and prepares for the ROAR of her life!

Roaaaar!

Lulu has done it! She managed to roar just when it mattered – the ground is beginning to rumble and shake. All the animals hear her warning roar for miles around!

The **flamingos** hear her and start to mutter to each other.

"Was that the little lion cub calling?"

"I think she's saying the volcano is erupting."

"Right, we need to fly!"

Stand up and reach one arm up to the sky.

Bend your leg up behind you. See if you can hold onto your foot.

Then try to hop, a bit like a tall, elegant flamingo.

33

The **snakes** slithering around hear Lulu.

Hssss hssss

"Sssounds like the lion cub."

Lie on the ground, on your tummy.

Wiggle your shoulders like a snake and go, "Hsssssss . . ."

Hssss hssss

Then place your hands under your shoulders and push yourself up.

"She isss roaring about a volcano erupting. Come sssnakesss, isss time to ssslither away!"

The **crocodiles** on the river bank hear her.

"Did you hear that?"

"Yes, I did. That was Lulu the lion cub."

"She says the volcano is going to blow. Let's get out of here and make it snappy!"

Lie on your side with your arms over your head.

Snap your crocodile jaws by opening and closing your arms.

35

The **camels** hear her too.

Sit up on your knees and put your hands on your lower back.

Push your hips forward and your chest up to the sky.

Brrrmmmpph
Brrrmmmpph

Blow a big raspberry.

Well, that's charming of the camels!

In fact, all the animals hear Lulu's warning roar, including her mum, her dad, her brothers and her sisters. They are so proud of their lion cub.

Lulu has learned how to roar at last . . . and along the way she has found out how to cope with getting angry and frustrated. And, most importantly, she has saved everyone from the volcano!

Now that our friend Lulu has learned to roar,
it's time for us to get out of here.

Oh look! Floating down toward us is a hot-air
balloon. That's how we are going to get home.

*Sit down
with crossed legs
and blow the
balloon up nice
and full.*

*Bring
your hands to
either side of
your mouth
and blow.*

*Slowly
stretch
your arms out
as your balloon
gets bigger.*

*When it's as
big as it can be,
start to rock gently
from side to side.*

As we float away in the balloon, it rocks some more in the wind . . .

Put your hands on the ground next to you. Gently push yourself from side to side.

Lean deeply at first and then less and less each time, until you come to a stop in the centre.

Look down and wave to Lulu and all the animals we met.

39

Let's lie back and take a moment to be still and calm after all that action.

As we relax, let's think about our amazing adventure with Lulu.

Lie down comfortably on your back, your feet apart and your arms a little away from your sides.

Feel your arms and legs become heavy and long. Melt into the ground and close your eyes to enjoy a rest and think about the yoga adventure you have been on.

Lulu got really angry and frustrated, didn't she?

Everyone has those feelings sometimes.
But it's good that we have ways of helping
ourselves so we don't end up doing something
mean, like tying poor Ernie's trunk in a knot!

We can practise things like breathing and counting
to help us feel calm again. Let's practise now and
breathe slowly . . .

We can always breathe ourselves into this calm place
– it's one of the amazing things we can learn in yoga
and use any time.

This is an affirmation. Affirmations are good and helpful thoughts that we say out loud.

When we say an affirmation, we make it come alive – like planting a seed and giving it sunshine and water. Then it grows into something big and strong that will help us in our life.

Thoughts can be very powerful things. When we turn them into affirmations they become even stronger.

As you lie on the floor, put one hand on your chest and one hand on your tummy and try saying the affirmation out loud.

Believe the words as you say them and they will grow stronger and stronger, until they are part of who you are.

Repeat the words a few times out loud. It doesn't have to be more than a whisper.

"I am calm and relaxed."

"With practice I can learn anything!"

Lulu also likes this affirmation. You can copy her or make up some good ones of your own.

We rest quietly in this peaceful time.
We have learned so much and
we have made such lovely friends,
especially Lulu the lion cub!

It's time to end our yoga adventure,
so let's sit up like we did at the beginning.

*Did you find Greg the grasshopper
hiding in every picture?*

Slowly start to wiggle your fingers and toes. Have a little stretch and then roll over to one side. Sit up slowly and cross your legs.

Bring your hands to your heart and bow forward, saying our special yoga code word, "Na-ma-stay".

Namaste!
Goodbye!

Jaime's top tips for using the Cosmic Kids books

Grown-ups, here are a few tips for helping children get the most out of the Cosmic Kids adventure books. It doesn't matter if you don't practise yoga yourself, you can still encourage your children to have a go at the poses – and you might want to have some fun trying them out for yourself!

Read the story, copy the moves and enjoy the adventure

This is an active book that encourages children to act out the story by doing the yoga moves. It's a lot of fun and provides children with a great, balanced yoga routine. They can come back to the book again and again, becoming more skilled and eventually developing their own yoga practice. After going on the yoga adventure a few times, they may even be able to do the whole routine, with all the poses in order, without looking at the book!

Start by reading the story and looking at the pictures

Being able to visualize the characters and understand what's happening in the story will help children as they try out the yoga moves.

Use a yoga mat (or a towel)

A yoga mat gives a soft surface to lie on, as well as a defined space to practise in. Plus it makes it feel like 'proper' yoga! If you don't have a mat, try using a rug or a big towel.

Taking part is more important than getting it right

Even though all the yoga poses in the book are adapted from traditional 'adult' yoga, the key is to make the experience as fun and playful for children as possible. So rather than stopping them to correct their poses, it's best to let the children interpret what they see and read and have fun making the shapes of the poses. With practice, as they re-read and look at the pictures again, they will become more accurate. The main goal is for them to enjoy the yoga!

Try to do each pose on both sides

This helps to keep the body in balance.

Join in to help the kids get the most out of their yoga adventure

- Make the animal noises! Encouraging the children to make fun sounds while they do the moves helps remind them of the poses.
- Get the children to come up with extra ideas for the story. You could ask them what the flamingos are called, for example, or what we need to pack to go on a camping trip.
- Bring the poses into everyday life. It's always a good time for a monkey jump! Or you might want to ssslither around like a snake, or hop like a flamingo, or snap like a crocodile . . .

Talk about the story

Each Cosmic Kids adventure offers practical advice for dealing with a particular issue. It's really useful to talk to your children about what they learned from the story so they have some ideas and techniques available when similar situations occur in real life. Ask the children if they can relate to any of the characters in the story and what they would do if something like that happened to them. Lulu shows how to deal with frustration and anger by doing something physical – yoga and breathing really help. Her other message is that we should keep trying and never give up on our dreams!

Practise the affirmations

These short statements are handy tools for daily life, helping to provide instant calm and also to sow the seeds for positive change (see pages 42–3).

Try out the video

You can watch and practise with me on the Cosmic Kids YouTube channel – access Lulu's adventure and many others via my website: www.cosmickids.com

Watch out for more Cosmic Kids books . . .

There are lots more yoga adventures to be had. You can dive down to the bottom of the ocean and help Norris the seahorse face up to the bullies. In the Wild West, Sheriff Updown the rabbit is in a spot of bother with the bandits – can his amazing Zappy Happy save the day? And Twilight the unicorn needs a hand delivering starshine to the magical Land of Sleep.

For Martin, Mini and Spence – and Cosmic Kids all over the world

Author acknowledgments

A huge thank you to Konrad Welz, Nick Hilditch and my super-talented husband Martin for the amazing work done behind the scenes at Cosmic Kids. Thank you so much Fiona Robertson, Jade Wheaton, Simona Sideri and the team at Watkins Publishing for getting behind these books and working hard to make them brilliant. Thank you David Lloyd, for taking such good photos. Thank you to teachers, parents and especially kids who have given me the inspiration to make these stories, and to our partnership team at YouTube for helping us keep Cosmic Kids yoga freely available to kids all over the world.

About Cosmic Kids

Jaime and Martin Amor are a husband-and-wife team from Henley-on-Thames who run Cosmic Kids with the aim of making yoga and mindfulness fun for kids. It all began in their local village hall in 2012, when they filmed a 'yoga adventure' Jaime had been sharing in her yoga classes in nearby schools. This was the first of many videos posted to YouTube and now – many monthly episodes later – millions of kids worldwide have discovered yoga and mindfulness through the free videos. Every Cosmic Kids yoga adventure is written to help kids learn a simple lesson for a happy life, so that they understand themselves and the world around them a little better.

To have more fun with Cosmic Kids, visit **cosmickids.com**!

Lulu the Lion Cub Learns to Roar
Jaime Amor

First published in the UK and USA in 2016 by
Watkins, an imprint of Watkins Media Limited
19 Cecil Court
London WC2N 4EZ

enquiries@watkinspublishing.com

Publisher: Jo Lal
Development Editor: Fiona Robertson
Editor: Simona Sideri
Head of Design: Viki Ottewill
Designer and Picture Research: Jade Wheaton
Production: Uzma Taj
Commissioned Illustration: Nick Hilditch
Commissioned Photography: Evolve Portraits

EVOLVE
portraits

A CIP record for this book is available from the
British Library

ISBN: 978-1-78028-957-1

10 9 8 7 6 5 4 3 2 1

Typeset in Museo Sans Rounded, Rockwell and
Caviar Dreams
Colour reproduction by XY Digital, UK
Printed in China

www.watkinspublishing.com